YAOIFIED LOVE

Z. ALLORA

ROCKY RIDGE BOOKS

Warning: this book contains adult language and themes, including graphic descriptions of sexual acts that some may find offensive. It is intended for mature readers only, of legal age to possess such material in their area.

This book is a work of fiction. All characters, companies, events, and locations are either products of the author's imagination or are used fictitiously. Any resemblance to actual persons, living or dead, places, or events is entirely coincidental and beyond the intent of the author and publisher.

Published by:

Rocky Ridge Books

PO Box 6922

Broomfield, CO 80021

http://RockyRidgeBooks.com

What they're saying about Z. Allora:

"Z. Allora writes individuals from her heart that grab the reader and won't let go, even after finishing the book." (Lock and Key)
    — Becky Condit, USA Today

"I really enjoyed this story... I would definitely recommend this book."
    —Rainbow Gold Book Reviews

"A sexy, steamy tale that keeps you turning the page to see what's going to happen next. (Zombies Ahead)
    –Mrs. Condit & Friends

"It was a great read, and I highly recommend it for those who enjoy BDSM and emotional stories." —The Novel Approach

"The scenes are heated and well written... I'm glad I had the opportunity to read the book..." —Joyfully Jay

To Ayano Yamane

Your scorching hot Viewfinder Series led me to the path
of Yaoi and my life has never been the same.
Much love & many thanks,
Z. Allora

Acknowledgments

To my twin: Felicia Y. Smith thank you for suggesting I might enjoy Ayano Yamane's work and meeting me at YaoiCon 2010!

Much appreciation to Desi for her mad editing skills.

To Laura R: We didn't meet in person yet you remain with me. May the bishies in heaven be sweet, sexy, and adorable.

Many thanks to Eden Winters for her patience reads and re-reads and blurb fixes, to TD O'Malley for not blowing smoke at me and yawning when I bore you, to Katie Obbink for proofing and encouraging my cameo, and to P.D. Singer for her overall magic.

A big thank you to Rocky Ridge Books who allows me the freedom to write everything that I need to write and share. Many hugs to all of you.

As always to my love for taking me to YaoiCon, for insisting my booth really needs a working penis cannon, and for finding interesting sites that make long drives so much more fun. You are my heart, my love and my life.

CHAPTER 1

"Oh my God! You totally look like Akihito from *Viewfinder*," a fan dressed as a schoolgirl squealed, waving her cell phone at him.

Rory Lewis scanned the hotel lobby. She was definitely talking to him. What should he do?

Amber, his best friend since fourth grade, elbowed him. "She wants a picture. Pose!" She jumped to the side.

"Sure." He grabbed the camera resting over his heart as if he were the actual photographer in his favorite manga, then gave the fan a half smile.

His pose must have worked, because the Yaoi fan clicked her phone and cried out, "Wow! Thank you!"

Amber patted him on the back. "See? Didn't I tell you YaoiCon would be awesome?"

Rory nodded. "I can't believe she knew who I was dressed as."

"I told you! You're his double, with your wide-eyed

innocence. Adding a camera and hair gel just Akihitoed you."

The *Viewfinder* series had been his gateway to Yaoi. He was enthralled by the tough mobster in lust, and probably in love, with a troublesome photographer who was always getting into dangerous situations. The mobster always rescued him... and the sex between them scorched the pages!

Rory had never admitted the depths of his love for this series, but somehow his bestie knew. Amber always understood things without him having to say, which made him love her even more.

Two guys strolled past, rocking pink cat ears and twitching tails.

"Did you see their tails? They moved—I bet we can buy some in the dealer's room." Amber nudged his shoulder.

Oh man, YaoiCon! He was at YaoiCon. He'd been anxious and almost backed out at the last minute. However, Amber tricked him by purchasing VIP tickets for his twentieth birthday. He couldn't insult her by not enjoying her present.

A group in sailor outfits waved as they skipped past. Everyone seemed friendly. Why had he waited? These were his people.

"There's Sangon! I want to talk to him." Amber ran off, abandoning him.

He stood in line and got his badge. "Thanks."

Rory spun around and slammed right into a solid chest. "Oops! Sorry."

He tried to step back, but strong hands grabbed his shoulders, steadied him, and kept him in place.

"I'm not." Mr. Tall, Dark, and Sexy, decked out in a pinstriped suit, gave him a crooked smile and an arched eyebrow. Damn, the guy was a dead ringer for Asami Ryuichi, Akihito's love interest in the *Viewfinder* series.

An "Aw, look!" rose from the crowd gathered around them. "It's Asami and Akihito!"

Squeals and "Look this way!" tried to pull Rory out of the depths of those dark eyes, but the rapid beat of his heart froze him. The man turned and grinned at the crowd.

Once everyone snapped pictures and dispersed, the guy released him. "I'm Kyle Austin."

Holy fuck! His deep voice sent shivers through Rory.

Amber appeared by Rory's side and nudged him, forcing him to spit out, "Um, I'm Rory Lewis."

"We'll probably bang... into each other a lot." The man's rich voice called to Rory's most submissive side and aroused him.

The "I hope so" got stuck in Rory's throat, so he nodded and watched Kyle glide to the front desk.

Amber leaned against him. "Wow, the back view is as hot as the front."

"Amber!" Rory shoved her.

Giving him her most virtuous expression, she demanded, "What? Tell me I'm wrong."

He couldn't. Those pants cupped Kyle's ass in a way....

"Come on. Time for the first panel on Why Yaoi."

3

She dragged Rory off in the opposite direction from where he wanted to follow Kyle. Wasn't there a question he needed to ask at the front desk? He couldn't resist one more peek over his shoulder and found Kyle's dark gaze staring back at him.

So fucking hot! A quiver of want ran through him.

"Earth to Rory." Amber waved a hand in front of his face.

The guy—like so many others Rory had met—was probably just a pretty face, and stupid wasn't sexy.

"Rory! Rory!" She shook him.

"Huh?" He refocused on his best friend. "What?"

"Come on, the first panel is this way." Amber dragged him to the line of costumed Yaoi attendees heading into the discussion room. They found seats toward the back.

Kyle breezed through the door and set a travel mug on the table at the front of the room. Rory's insides clenched. Jesus, his confident, take-charge attitude made Rory weak in the knees.

Kyle called everyone to attention. "Good morning. You're here for the Why Yaoi discussion? What do we love?"

"Yaoi," most of the fans said quietly.

"I can't hear you! Isn't this YaoiCon? What do we love?"

Everyone roared. "Yaoi!"

"Better. I'm Kyle Austin and a senior in college. I'm doing this panel as part of my thesis... on Yaoi."

The crowd whooped and clapped.

Kyle put his palm out as if to soothe the crowd into

silence. "What I'm going to share here today is simply my opinion and some theories. I've based this discussion on the subjective information I've gathered attending Yaoi-Cons, speaking to some of you, reading a fuckton of Yaoi, and chatting on the boards."

He took a quick sip from his travel mug and paced in front of the table. "Much of this is a vast generalization. Keep in mind that the world is fluid and ever-changing."

"Wow, Kyle, that's some disclaimer. Do you think we're going to take you to court?" Rory couldn't see the guy giving Kyle shit, but he hoped the jackass was done.

Shrugging, Kyle continued, "I'll be handing out a survey later. If you're interested in being part of it, I'd welcome your input."

A guy dressed as a schoolboy snarked, "I'll take your input... deep."

"Out of curiosity, how many of us here are on the rainbow?" Kyle raised his own hand.

Amber grabbed Rory's hand and held it up with her own.

Rory smiled at the sea of waved palms.

A blonde wearing a beret in the fifth row called out, "I'm genderqueer of the transmasculine variety. And I think that's partly why I was drawn to Yaoi."

A large number of people raised their hands and nodded in agreement.

One of a group of six that were dressed in swim trunks, zippered jackets, and goggles around their necks like the guys in *Free! Iwatobi Swim Club* raised his hand. "Transguy here. Totally get that."

"I'm agender," a person Rory couldn't see called out.

A voice in the back said, "I'm a lesbian and my girl-friend is asexual. We both love Yaoi."

Kyle nodded. "Thank you for sharing. Visibility is important. I think there are many reasons why people are drawn to Yaoi."

After taking a quick sip from his mug, Kyle continued. "There's not a lot of time to explore this, but another facet of this puzzle is some people assigned female at birth don't identify as such, and these characters allow them to better understand themselves."

The blond in the beret said, "That's true for me. I loved romance novels, but I never identified with the female characters. Then I discovered Yaoi... and well, wow."

Rory had never read romance novels, though Amber had said she adored reading m/m romance.

Someone cosplaying Yurio from *Yuri on Ice* who had sparkly ice skates sitting in front of them as if they just came from practice admitted, "It helped me explore my gender identity too."

The trans-guy group nodded along with several other people in the audience.

Kyle smiled at the audience. "Thank you for sharing. Yaoi can be a path for some to understand themselves better. Okay, now as great as Yaoi is in allowing some of us to explore sexuality, in many cases the Yaoi characters themselves don't come out. There's a lack of admission, honesty, and acceptance of being gay in Yaoi—which is fucked."

Rory wasn't surprised by the groans, but he was happy about mumblings of affirmation. Admitting there was an issue was the first thing that needed to happen in terms of addressing it.

"I agree with the criticism," Kyle continued. "However, when I look at the Japanese culture, I can't help but wonder if that's more about where they are in their understanding of LGBTQIA."

The person with rainbow hair and cat ears raised their hand, and asked, "What do you mean?"

"Well, the places where LGBTQIA people are accepted didn't do so immediately. There were growing pains, marches, education.... I'm not saying this to justify the lack of coming out in Yaoi, only to give a possible explanation. Some people might not have the experience or verbiage to do the subject of coming out justice. Or to even express themselves."

Why hadn't Rory thought about that? It was true.

"And think about how LGBTQIA people were first presented in books and movies here in America. Not that long ago it was rare to see anyone who wasn't straight as anything more than a joke, and none of the early romances ended happily."

"It was all death, dying or murder," someone nearby muttered.

Kyle shrugged. "Society is evolving...."

Rory could listen to him speak all day. Kyle was interesting and smart, and the cadence of his deep voice relaxed and excited Rory all at once.

Kyle's gaze connected to Rory's, making him squirm

in his seat and wish he'd have the opportunity to get to know Kyle better.

The lecture continued, discussing the progress that could be seen in various Yaoi, but Rory just watched his liquid movements and enjoyed the way his voice wrapped around him.

"There's still a long way to go, but you can see the growth within the genre. As wonderful as *Junjo Romanica* is it fails throughout the story to address and accept homosexuality, the sports anime *Yuri On Ice* has a gay relationship but it's in the background. The love between the characters is simply accepted. The relationship is presented as a small piece of the story and in a normalizing not sensationalizing way."

Clapping his hands, Kyle said, "Let's go back to the original question: Why do we love Yaoi?"

Lots of answers were shouted out, but Rory said, "Because we do."

Kyle zoned in on him. "That's right. We each have our own personal and unique reasons why Yaoi calls to us... and we're here answering that call. We love Yaoi because we do."

The room burst into applause.

Wow, just wow! Rory stood and clapped with everyone else in the room. He shifted, and tried adjusting his pants without anyone noticing how tight they'd gotten.

Kyle waved a stack of forms. "Fill out one of these or go online and file one at www.yaoiwtf.com. Thanks so much, and have a great Con."

Amber elbowed Rory and handed him a tissue.

He stared at the flowery paper. "What's this for?"

She whispered, "You're drooling."

Rory balled the tissue and tossed it at her face. "Am not!" He wiped the corner of his lips just to be sure. "He's just so—"

"Yummy? You should talk to him," Amber whispered. "You know, and maybe finally explore the other side of your *bisexuality*."

Rory glared.

Why couldn't he be like her? She was free, sexually expressive, and perceived new experiences as something to relish. Ah, to be half as open! But getting knocked around in high school for being different probably beat the carefree out of him.

Though who was he kidding? Even in college, he wasn't comfortable being unguarded.

Rory glanced to the front of the room.

Fans swarmed Kyle, but his gaze landed on Rory and locked. Kyle gave him a smile that turned Rory's insides upside down and made him readjust his wants list.

"He keeps staring at you. Go talk to him," Amber hissed and nudged his arm.

Rory would love to talk to Kyle, but he couldn't.... Could he? He went for indignant. "And say what?"

Amber's grin told him he'd failed. "You'll think of something, Rory. This is YaoiCon! He's here, you're here. Clearly you have something in common."

Rory doubted he could have much in common with the gorgeous man, but fuck! He could've listened to Kyle read a fast-food restaurant menu and it would've given him wood. He needed to get a grip... and not on that.

People were drifting out of the room, and Amber said, "I'm going to run to the restroom before the Genderqueer & Yaoi panel."

A girl with pink hair noticed Rory lingering. "You look so much like him!" She grabbed Rory's hand and tugged him to the front of the room. "Please! Take a picture with Kyle for me!"

Oh God!

Kyle shrugged. He tugged Rory close and purred, "So we meet again."

Rory took pride that he didn't whimper when the pictures were taken, but it was a close thing. The way Kyle's breath tickled his ear and.... Good Lord, he smelled incredible, like... man.

"Hug him!" a fan shouted.

Strong, sculpted arms encompassed Rory and hauled him against Kyle's front. How was he supposed to hold it together? Kyle rested his chin on Rory's shoulder and whispered, "You were made for me."

Someone toting a ton of books and merchandise from a second group of fans who spilled through the open door asked, "Can you sit on the table with him between your legs?"

Swallowing, Rory glanced at Kyle, who spared him a smirk sexy enough to make the devil blush.

Kyle clasped his hands around Rory's waist, and— whoosh! He tossed him right onto the table.

Oh God! Kyle trailed his hands down to Rory's knees,

held firm, and then in one smooth move pushed them open. *Yes!* Kyle was as dominant as the mobster he cosplayed.

Welcoming Kyle between the V of his legs felt undeniably right.

Kyle nestled close. His erection nudged Rory's.

Fucking hell! Kyle caressed his palms along Rory's thighs.

He wouldn't whimper and beg. But the knowledge that with just a little shifting, they'd be rubbing off on each other tormented him. He'd never been this close to another guy before, especially not boned up.

The photographers moaned.

Breathless, Rory gazed at Kyle. Want, need, and lust passed between them, but there was something more. Some unnamed understanding or emotion Rory dare not name. Was it possible that Kyle felt the chemistry too?

Everything Rory had been waiting for seemed to be right here, accessible....

If Kyle were to push Rory onto his back—

"Hey, let's give them a good picture." Kyle licked his thumb, and brushed the wetness across Rory's lower lip, dragging his mouth open.

Yes! He'd give Kyle whatever he wanted. Rory's world shrunk down to the man in front of him. The camera and cellphone clicks became distant. The other fans disappeared.

Rory had to be closer. He wrapped his legs around Kyle's ass, and pulled him in until he was flush.

Mmmm, they were hard-on to hard-on. At least Rory

wasn't the only one aroused. He'd been with girls, but he'd never found a guy he wanted to—

Kyle cupped Rory's cheek. The move secured and tilted Rory's head. The angle gave him a view of Kyle's tongue swiping out, tracing moisture over his own perfect lips, leaving them glistening and oh-so-kissable.

Desire slashed through Rory. Never before had he craved a kiss the way he yearned for Kyle's. He'd finally get to taste a guy's mouth, and not just any guy's, but *Kyle's*. Just an inch away—

But lips never met lips. Kyle stopped his descent.
What? No!

Rory panted and fastened his hands onto Kyle's trim waist. He tried to pull him closer, but Kyle remained frozen.

Mountain Dew breath teased Rory's lips, making him crave the sweetness that remained out of his reach.

Rory should close the distance, he should—

Kyle turned his head away in slow motion and told the group, "That's all. The next panel is about to start."

Disappointment crushed Rory.

What had he been thinking? Of course, this guy wouldn't be interested in him. Fans were just taking pictures. Jesus, was Rory so pathetic he couldn't see the difference? This was cosplay, emphasis on *play*. Guys got hard all the time. Besides, Kyle probably had a boyfriend... or boyfriends!

Rory dropped his hands and clenched them into fists. He wouldn't reach out and drag Kyle to his mouth. He might not have a lot of experience, but he did have some pride.

He pushed Kyle back and jumped to the floor, then rejoined a wide-eyed Amber. "Come on. It's time for the next panel."

"Rory," Kyle called out to him.

He didn't stop. He couldn't. He towed Amber in his wake. Rory waved without looking. "Catch you later, Kyle."

At lunch, Amber decided room service was a viable option, but the hotel kitchen must have been overwhelmed with the convention. It took forever to get food, which was fine because Rory was relieved to spend a good chunk of the afternoon in their room.

Not that he was avoiding anyone in particular; he wanted to enjoy the hotel room before the rest of the evening's festivities began.

Amber seemed to almost believe him.

CHAPTER 2

Rory glanced around the huge ballroom filled with Yaoi fans. "So, what's Bishie Bingo again?"

"It's like bingo. . but way more!" Amber's eyes sparkled, hinting at what the *more* might be.

Would Kyle be participating? Not that Rory cared. "Amber, do we have to sit so close to the stage?"

She sighed. "Yes, I want to get lots of bingo cards and a good view. There are some great prizes!"

"Like what?" Rory squinted at the prize table on stage.

"There's boxed sets, original prints, signed copies of books, DVDs, and a bunch of other great stuff. Plus, you get to remove an item of clothing from a bishie boy!" She giggled.

A fan wearing a blue wig leaned over and said, "Hi, I'm Laura. Couldn't help but overhear. This is from last year's event."

She held her phone out and played a video clip of someone ripping off a blushing bishie's pirate shirt.

"Um, thanks." Rory glared at Amber.

Laura gave him a sweet smile and proclaimed, "Bishie Bingo is live Yaoi." She turned back to chat with her friend.

Amber waved him off. "What? See? It's only one item of clothing."

Rory wiped a hand over his face. "There're so many things wrong with that statement...."

Laura's friend giggled. "You're too funny."

Rory shrugged and then tried to figure what the aqua beret was about. "I'm sorry, I don't recognize the beret. Which character are you?"

"I'm me. It's what I do best."

"Outstanding I—" He grinned. "Ow!"

Amber removed her elbow from his side and squealed, "It's starting."

He turned his attention to the stage.

The announcer—wearing black leather, a white pirate's shirt, and carrying a crop—mounted the stairs two at a time. His long hair was secured in chopsticks. He stalked to center stage as he waved to the audience. "Good evening! I'm Raven, and I'll be your host for tonight. Let's welcome our bishies!"

Scantily clad and costumed men took the stage, and the audience jumped to their feet. Rory wasn't sure, but the standing ovation seemed to be more about getting a better view than anything else.

"There's Kyle." Amber elbowed Rory in the arm.

Kyle jogged to the top of the stairs, stepped in line, and folded his arms. He had on his suit but the crisp white shirt was half-open. A piece of dark hair curled down on his forehead as he gave the audience a superior, mobster glare.

"Um, yeah." Rory shivered. *Why is he so fucking stunning?*

"Our beautiful bishies will be *coming*...." The announcer purred the last word, ensuring the crowd roared.

Rory glanced around. Damn, would this mob rush the stage? Nah, this was YaoiCon. The fans were just enthusiastic, right?

The announcer grinned. "Yes, they'll be... *coming*, and so will you... if you're lucky."

Another round of giggling and clapping echoed through the ballroom.

He waved a paddle emblazoned with the word "YAOI" etched in glitter. "Enough. Don't make me use this in a bad way."

Someone shouted, "*Is* there a bad way?"

The announcer feigned a glare and growled, "Don't try me. Now, as I was saying, the bishies will... *strut, wiggle, and sashay* among the hordes of you fans so you may purchase bingo cards."

Rory surveyed the stage. All the guys were lined up like some smoking-hot man buffet. One had only a loin-cloth and carried a vine, another dressed in a sailor outfit, and another was decked out like a pirate. Some were recognizable characters, several others were in leather, and one wore a frilly maid's outfit complete with fishnets and heels. But none compared to Kyle.

Kyle had donned not only a tailored pinstriped suit but a "fuck you" attitude as well. He stood there, mobster casual, and conveyed his readiness to screw or kill at a moment's notice.

Shit! It was crazy to stare at someone who could have stepped out of Rory's masturbatory dreams. God, Rory wanted... to buy a card from him.

The bishies leapt off the stage and rushed into the crowd. Kyle was almost assaulted by fans anxious to flirt shamelessly with him as they purchased cards. He seemed to take the attention in stride and gave back clever one-liners. Watching him zigzag through the crowd, their eyes locked.

Kyle's frown turned into a small sexy smile. He mouthed, "I'll be right there."

Was he talking to Rory? God, Rory could almost believe Kyle might be attempting to work his way over to him.

What a sight! The perfect cut of his suit clung in all the right places. His open shirt exposed his throat, and a hint of chest hair.

Rory held out his money, but before Kyle could take it, another bishie, dressed in Chinese armor, snatched the cash with a grin and handed over a card.

Drat! Rory could buy another card, but that would appear desperate.

Kyle shrugged, smiled, and winked before he moved on to the next fan flashing cash.

The announcer called out, "Last call, lovelies. Buy a card from one of our harem of bishies. But hurry, the game is about to start."

When the last bishie returned to the stage, the game started. Bingo moved at a fast pace—until the winners started to collect their prizes. Then the tempo dropped to the same rate Yaoi was translated into English... *too slow*.

Rory whispered his frustration to Amber. "Why do all the winners focus on Kyle? There are other guys up there."

She shrugged. "Well, maybe they, like you, want to get your Kyle naked."

"He's not my Kyle!"

"Oh really? Look, your Mr. Sexy in Mob-wear is fun and playful with the winners."

God, Kyle's undress-me attitude bordered on inappropriate. Rory pressed his lips together so he didn't say "*Too* playful!"

And the winners? *Man!* No one really needed to run their hands over someone's ass to remove wingtips— simply untie the fucking laces. No need to get all handsy.

During the fourth round, the MC reminded the winners they could enlist the help of other bishies in claiming the clothing item. "You'd get a two-for-one, and some of our bishies *really like* each other."

What the hell was he implying? Kyle might have a boyfriend who is a bishie? No way could Rory compete with that sexy confidence!

The very next winner must have decided the announcer had made a great point. She whispered to a bishie wearing a cutoff football jersey, protective padding that made his shoulders look huge, cleats, and white pants so tight they looked painted on. He nodded to her, grinned at the audience, and then stood in front of Kyle.

Of course!

The football player said something Rory couldn't make out and tugged a reluctant Kyle front and center.

The MC said, "Hands behind your back, Kyle-san."

Kyle scowled, but did as requested.

The football player started to unbutton Kyle's shirt.

The announcer asked, "Can't you be more creative? Come on, Leon. We all know *how* imaginative you are...."

Words passed between Kyle and the football player. The bishie untucked Kyle's shirt, and ran his fingers along the buttons. He bent and, with his teeth, opened the buttons one at a time.

Once the shirt was undone, there was truly no need for the bishie to run his tongue over Kyle's chest. Regardless of what the screaming, gleeful fans thought. Tongue baths shouldn't be part of Bingo!

Was Kyle enjoying the attention or hamming his reactions up for the audience? He gasped when the bishie bit his nipple, making Rory wish he'd been the cause of that erotic sound.

It had to be a conspiracy because every one of the winners continued to focus on undressing Kyle. They slipped his belt off.

The announcer put the leather to use on the bishie dressed as a maid. The maid took the belting right over his frilly panties. The sight made Rory tremble. This really was like walking through a live Yaoi!

The next winner was an attractive man in his thirties. He strutted down the aisle and jumped onto the stage like he owned it. As soon as his bingo card was verified, the winner pointed at Kyle. "Kyle, if you please."

He led Kyle to the center of the stage, and unbuttoned Kyle's pants. Glancing over his shoulder, he asked the crowd, "More?"

The audience screamed, "Yes!"

The guy traced his fingers along Kyle's zipper. "Should I?"

Another affirmative roar rose to deafening levels.

The winner teased the crowd and, by all appearances, Kyle—by trailing his fingers around the waistband of the pants. "Do you think these should to come off?"

"Of course!" and "Please," along with "Yes!" rang out.

He hooked his fingers into Kyle's pants.

Someone nearby moaned. "The winner used to be my favorite bishie when he performed."

No wonder the guy was completely comfortable on stage. He was an accomplished tormentor and proved it as he gradually lowered Kyle's pants.

The announcer ordered, "Be so kind as to do a 360, Kyle."

Kyle stepped out of his pants.

The maid rushed to gather the pants off the floor, then folded them over a chair.

Doing a slow turn allowed Rory to ponder the interesting lines of fabric that intersected over Kyle's ass connected to a thong, creating an illusion of underwear, but more skin than cloth seemed to be revealed.

When Kyle faced the audience again, the announcer clapped. "Well done, Kyle-san. Well done."

The winner of the round dropped to his knees in front of Kyle, pretending—or at least Rory *hoped* he pretended—to blow Kyle. His head bobbed, and he grabbed Kyle's ass. He snuck his fingers under the material and touched skin.

Kyle combed his fingers through the winner's hair, threw his head back, and groaned.

Jesus, Rory didn't know which was worse: the irrational jealousy of someone touching Kyle or wanting to be the one to make him give those fucking sexy groans... or knowing he could never be that free.

Rory decided he was exhausted. "I'm heading to bed."

Amber made a face at him. "Alone?"

"No, with my two hands." He stomped down the aisle. The screaming crowd would cover his escape.

CHAPTER 3

Rory hadn't slept well, but he was determined to begin day two of YaoiCon with a fresh perspective. Deeming his crush silly, he'd just focus on fun, and no one would stop him. He threw the camera strap over his head and stood in front of the mirror to *Akihito* his hair a bit.

"Come on. I'm hungry!" Amber insisted.

They grabbed muffins in the hotel bakery. At the cashier, she eyed the Mountain Dew he'd added to their carb feast. "What's with the Dew?"

Not wanting to go there, he shrugged. "Trying something different."

She didn't have to know he was hoping to quell his need to experience the flavor. It had nothing to do with Kyle's mouth smelling of it.

All the chairs were taken in the lobby, so they found a place and leaned against the wall. Just as Rory was about to take a bite of the muffin, the elevator doors slid open.

Kyle strutted out of the elevator into the lobby... in a

towel. He wore only a motherfucking piece of terrycloth draped around his waist. The towel even dipped a bit in the front, revealing a dusting of dark hair that continued under the towel.

Rory's fingers itched to follow the trail and see what treasure he could find. Or maybe he'd just stroke his hands over the muscular chest that appeared slightly oiled. He could—

Rory lost control of his packaged blueberry muffin. The baked good hit the floor and rolled ten feet away. "Fuck me!"

"I bet if you asked him nice he would...," Amber snorted. Clearly not feeling the earth shift under her feet the way Rory did.

Kyle bent to snatch the wayward breakfast off the rug and then beelined over to Rory and Amber.

Goddamn it!

Rory remained because he couldn't disengage from Amber's grip without causing a scene.

"I think you dropped this." Kyle set the muffin into Amber's hand, since there was no way Rory would accept anything from him. Not even a kiss... and that definitely wasn't on offer. Kyle's lips were only available to other bishie boys.

"Oh my God! An Asami shower scene picture," someone shrieked. "Push Akihito against the wall."

Rory's traitorous ex-best friend slipped away, deserting him.

"Sounds good to me." Kyle grabbed Rory by the shoulders, and pressed against him. He trailed his fingers down Rory's arms until he interlocked their fingers.

Rory tried to glare at him, but his body absorbed the contact and leaned into the heat Kyle's mostly naked body gave off.

"And let's go all the way." In a quick move, Kyle yanked Rory's hands above his head and pinned them to the wall.

"Oh," Rory gasped.

The pose put Kyle in the dominant position. *Fuck!* It pushed all of Rory's buttons, and he couldn't deny going all the way sounded like a brilliant idea.

Frowning, Kyle said, "I couldn't find you after bingo last night."

He looked for me? So what? The defiance Rory could feel in his expression had nothing to do with playing a role of reluctance. "Maybe I didn't want to be found."

Someone in the crowd asked, "How are you this morning, Kyle?"

"Great. I'm with my little Rory here," Kyle purred with a hint of a Japanese accent.

Dammit! How many fantasies was this guy going to dangle in front of Rory before denying him?

"I'm not your anything." Rory banged his head against the wall. He surrendered to his fate and let the scene play out.

Kyle growled and took Rory's submissive move as an invitation. He traced his lips over Rory's throat, up and down, and then nipped along the base of his neck. His hold on Rory tightened.

A moan fell from Rory's lips. God, he hated his longing to be overpowered by Kyle for real, held hostage in the shower while Kyle took advantage of everything Rory yearned to give him.

Gentle suction threatened to leave a mark.

Shit! Rory craved a hickey, to carry Kyle's mark. His need to be Kyle's uke wasn't rational.

He almost pressed closer. No! It was too much. His cock had already gone hard, responding to Kyle's half-naked body rubbing against his.

How many times had he jerked off to the idea of someone holding him, forcing him... not quite non-con but overcoming his resistance? *Ha! He was the star of his own Yaoi.*

He panted and wished he had an ounce of anything less than enthusiasm where Kyle was concerned.

Kyle groaned and pushed closer. "I really wanted to see you last night."

Images of friendly bishies touching Kyle worked better than ice water to cool his ardor. Rory didn't bother to keep the irritation out of his voice when he asked, "For what? Looked like you had your own harem onstage."

"I've known those guys for years. Most of them have girlfriends or boyfriends...." Kyle grinned. "Wait, are you jealous?"

"I'm no such thing." Rory struggled to break free of the ironclad grip, but Kyle held him in place. His traitorous cock throbbed at being secured, and his favorite fantasy of playing a reluctant uke surfaced.

Kyle shifted, thrusting a knee between Rory's legs. "I think—"

The clearing of a throat wrenched Rory out of the depths of Kyle's dark brown eyes.

"Sir, you can't be in the lobby in a towel," a man in hotel uniform scolded.

With exaggerated slowness, Kyle released Rory's hands.

The crowd had increased in size. Some were still snapping pictures and maybe taking video. Shit, Rory would wind up on YouTube or Vine for sure.

Kyle stepped back and teased his fingers where the towel wrapped around him. How Rory wished to touch the smooth, warm skin. Agile fingers played in the folds of the fluffy white towel. He wasn't going to—

With a deft flick of his wrist, the wrap dropped to the floor.

The crowd inhaled, then exhaled with chuckles.

Rory wished he could find the board shorts Kyle wore humorous, but not even the Yaoi characters in odd pairings could make Rory laugh. No, unfortunately Rory envisioned slipping them down Kyle's hips, thighs, and legs, and—

"Just wanted to take a dip." The innocence in Kyle's voice astounded Rory.

"Um, sorry, sir, but our pool closes after Labor Day." The hotel employee didn't buy the excuse any more than Rory did.

"That's disappointing." Kyle ran his hand through his perfectly styled hair and never took his gaze off Rory.

Enough! Rory found Amber off to the side chatting with a guy, grabbed her hand, and fled into the dealer's room, hoping to get lost in the aisles of merchandise.

During lunch, Kyle slid into the chair Amber had just vacated.

"I'll be back." She gave Rory a wink and abandoned him.

Kyle leaned toward him. "Hey, I... wanted to say hi."

Was this actually happening? Rory's stomach knotted. "Hi."

"Hi...." Kyle's deep voice wrapped around Rory, pushing dark fantasies to the forefront of his mind.

Kyle stroked a single finger along the back of Rory's hand up his arm to the crease of his elbow, sending shivers of want through him with every stroke.

Rory shook his head, hoping to dislodge the desire of slipping to his knees, and—the mischievous sparkle in Kyle's eyes suggested he was well aware of how he tortured Rory. *Fuck!*

"Are you having a good Con?" Kyle's easygoing style said he did this all the time. This was no big deal to him.

Rory hated that Kyle's crooked smile had the power to make him melt. His anxiety dragged him into fight-or-flight mode. He pulled his arm away and chose fight. "Yeah. You looked like *you* were having fun last night."

Kyle shrugged. "I was in high school theater, and I try to play it up for the audience."

"Right." Totally out of Rory's league. Flight mode kicked in, forcing him to cut bait and run. He stood. "Well, good chatting with you. I've got to go."

"Oh, um, okay. I hope I see you again."

Argh! He needed to stop being so damned nice.

Rory ignored Kyle's frown and his own need to turn it into a smile. He waved and took off across the restaurant. He jogged down the stairs away from Kyle and his own stupid wants and needs... though his damned insecurities trailed after him all the way back to the hotel room.

As soon as Amber returned, Rory hated himself for asking, but he had to know. "So, who won Kyle?"

Rory had refused to go with her to the Bishie Auction. He'd had more than enough stress looking over his shoulder trying to avoid more encounters with Kyle all day long. After being depressingly successful, he couldn't bear the thought of watching someone bid on and buy time with Kyle.

"Unzip me," Amber begged. "I have to change. I'm going to Sangon's room for some adult fun."

He figured she'd be hooking up with the guy she'd been stalking all weekend. Doing her bidding, Rory repeated, "Who won Kyle?"

"No one. When I didn't see him there, I asked around, figuring you'd want to know."

Rory gave a lame denial. "I don't."

Shrugging, Amber huffed out, "Okay. Then I won't tell you what I know."

"Jackass." He glared.

"Says the guy who sat in our room all night and pouted." She must have taken pity on him and became serious. "Apparently, Kyle's father was in a car accident, so he flew home this afternoon before the auction even started."

"That's terrible!"

Amber nodded. "I heard his dad was in pretty bad shape, and poor Kyle was a mess."

Shit. Reality hit. Rory didn't have Kyle's contact information. "Does anyone have his email or social media details?"

Shaking her head, Amber said, "I asked, but Kyle is focused on finishing his degree, so he doesn't have any he shares."

"No social media?" His heart whined. *But we had a connection!* And his dick assured him they hadn't connected, only tormented each other with erotic suggestions.

It was nuts, but Rory really liked the guy, and now he'd lost his chance. Regret overwhelmed him.

"There's always next year...." Amber slipped out the door, escaping the pillow directed at her head.

Damn! Just damn!

CHAPTER 4

Bang! Bang! Bang!

"Rory! Rory! Are you back yet?" Was Amber going to break down his dorm door?

"Yeah, I just got in." He stepped over his suitcase filled with clean clothing—thanks to his mom—and pushed the door handle to let Amber into his dorm room.

She burst in like a tsunami. "Why didn't you respond to my texts over the break?"

"After Thanksgiving dinner, my sister's little girl thought my cell phone should take a bath. I couldn't face the crowds on Black Friday, so I figured I'd go to the phone store when I got back here. My dad got the protection plan on it so no biggie. Did you miss me?"

Rory moved his backpack and started to pull down the turkey hands Amber had pasted all over his dorm room to get him in the mood for the holidays.

Waving at his computer, she asked, "Did you check your email?"

"No phone, so no. And this dinosaur is still booting up." Hopefully, his parents took the hints and coupons he'd left for the laptop he wanted to replace his huge out-of-date desktop.

She stared at him as if trying to see if something was different or out of place. "How'd your date go?"

After YaoiCon she bullied him into joining a bunch of sites, and going out with guys. "Ah, you want to know how Operation Get Rory Boy-Laid is going?"

"Yeah."

He shook his head and exhaled hard. "As good as the last three you pushed me to go on."

Two of them had been nice guys, although there had been no chemistry. The third date was with an older man. While he was hot, he confessed to being in a complex poly relationship that seemed more confusing than sexy to Rory. And last night's date disaster simply creeped Rory out.

"Good."

"Good? This from the girl who made me get an account on Men4SexNow?" He rarely opened the app because it was unnerving to see the number of men searching for a hookup in close proximity to him.

"That's where you found the guy you met last night, right?"

He didn't grimace, but only great restraint prevented it. "Who would make the first question they ask a complete stranger, have you ever fucked a heated grapefruit?"

"And?"

"What? No, I never fucked a warmed grapefruit!" Her quizzical stare complete with head tilt made him clarify. "Or any other fruit or vegetable."

She rolled her eyes. "Well, you shouldn't discount cucumbers. I—"

"Never mind. I don't want to know." He'd bet money on having to endure the story about her and intimate relations with a cucumber during their next game of I Never.

His prehistoric computer groaned readiness, and she exclaimed, "Finally! Now go to the YaoiCon page."

His heart triple-timed. It couldn't be, but she was so gleeful he hoped for the impossible.

There was a countdown post to next year's convention with details about the hotel. Several people posted video clips, and a number of pictures of the antics. He glanced over his shoulder at her.

She gestured him onward. "Scroll down."

There for all to see was a meme of half-naked Kyle in a towel holding Rory's hands above his head. It read: *Seme needs to find his uke. If you have any information, please contact me.*

"Holy fuck!" Kyle was looking for him? He stared at Amber to make sure he wasn't getting this wrong.

"I know! Several jackasses left comments about offering uke service to him, but I messaged him directly."

There had to be a trick. "It might not be him. This could be someone catfishing me."

"No, I think it's him. He had too many details and said he'd email you. Go check." She waved with wild abandon at the screen.

Right there at the top of his account were two new emails. He opened the top one, sent three hours ago. The subject line read: *Sorry.*

Rory,

Maybe you think I'm a stalker and that's why you haven't responded. I get it. If I don't hear from you, I won't pursue you.

-Kyle

"Shit! Rory!" Amber stopped leaning over his shoulder and typed on her phone. "There. I told him you'd broke your phone and you'd Skype him as soon as you were settled."

"What?"

Amber grabbed him by the shoulders and spun him around in his desk chair to face her. "Best friend to best friend. You sparked with him. He likes you. Read his other email, and Skype him when you're ready."

He nodded.

"I'm going to visit Doug. See you tomorrow for class, and the dirty details. Text—Skype me if you need me." She slipped out of his room.

He locked his door and paced. This could be classified as crazy. He couldn't believe Kyle had looked for him. Although afraid, curiosity got the better of him. Sitting at his computer, he read the first email Kyle had sent.

Hey, Rory!

I'm sorry I didn't get to exchange contact information with you. My dad was in a car crash and was in critical condition for several weeks. He's doing better, though I've been slammed at school trying to catch up, but over break I thought I'd see if you.... Look, I'm not going to play it cool. I like you. I can't stop thinking about you. I want to get to know you better. My Skype is KyleAustin28.

-Kyle

Rory reread the email twice. He slowed down each time on the "I like you," and "I can't stop thinking about you" parts. For some reason, Rory brushed his teeth, changed his T-shirt to a plain black one, and ran some product through his hair.

Skype's video chat connected while he was wiping his hands on his pants. Shit! He hadn't embellished Kyle's looks one bit. If anything, his memory paled in comparison.

"Hey, Rory. Sorry for hunting you down, but... well, you read the email, right?"

Rory nodded. After staring like he didn't have use of his mouth, he finally asked, "How's your father?"

"Better. He's still got some surgeries and physical therapy, but he's strong." Kyle leaned in closer to the screen and gave Rory a deadly smile. "So, what's your favorite Yaoi trope?"

And just like that, they were off and chatting until midnight.

At Christmas break, Rory stayed at school an extra day to Skype with Kyle. Hopefully, his parents had gotten him a laptop for Christmas. He and Kyle stayed connected by a running text every few minutes, which was new and wonderful to Rory because they'd decided to stick with email until exams were done.

On Christmas Eve, Rory's parents gave him his present early. It was a laptop, and with the help of Kyle via phone, Rory got it set up and was skyping in no time.

A minute after midnight, Kyle said, "Hey, check your email."

Rory stifled a yawn and clicked over to his email. A Christmas card from Kyle waited for him. Attached was a plane ticket confirmation from California to Rhode Island in March. "What's this?"

"Meet me at BishounenCon."

"What?"

"You said you don't have class on Fridays next semester. We can spend the whole weekend together."

"Kyle...." How could he even think about accepting such an extravagant gift?

"Merry Christmas, Rory." Kyle gave him a heart flipping smile over Skype. "Make my holiday and say you'll join me."

How could he not? "Merry Christmas. Thank you so much. I can't wait to see you."

"Me too."

"So, you're not going to Skype with him until when?"

Rory smirked. "Well, we decided as long as we got

our work done during the week we could have a Skype date on Saturday night."

"Sweet! Skype sex is safe sex."

"What? It's not like that."

"Whatever you say." Amber's giggle clearly stated her disbelief.

"Do you always have to turn my every action into the dirtiest Yaoi ever?"

"Um, wait, let me look up the answer." She paged through her invisible best friend book she always pretended to drag out. "Yup. It looks like I do. It's right there on page forty-eight."

"Jackass."

"Me the jackass? You're not even chatting with your boyfriend—"

"He's not my boyfriend."

"Say what now?"

"We agreed not to label what we're doing." It made practical sense.

Rory felt mature to be the one to insist on that. He'd made Kyle promise they wouldn't discuss anything about their future plans either.

———

"Happy Valentine's Day, Rory." The words pulled him from sleep, but because they were from Kyle, he didn't mind.

Sun streamed through Rory's dorm window. He

stared at the laptop screen. "We must have fallen asleep on Skype again."

Kyle stretched and finger-combed his hair while he smiled at his computer screen. "We did." He pulled off his T-shirt.

Holy Mother of Manga! Rory wished he wasn't across the country. The things he wanted to try. He reached down and straightened his morning wood. With this kind of visual, it was no wonder his cock was even more rearing to go than usual.

"Rory?" Kyle shifted on his bed. He ran his hand down his chest, and stopped just above the navy-blue sheet that covered his lower half.

Rory shifted and realized he still held on to his dick. "Kyle?"

"You wanna?"

He could play dumb but.... "If you don't think it's weird, then hell yes."

"Oh, thank the gods of cyberspace." Kyle pulled down his sheet, revealing a pair of red underwear with a blue band at the top. Reaching inside, he gripped his cock and gave it a stroke. The glistening tip poked out of his waistband.

Rory scrambled to kick out of his pajama bottoms and caressed his naked dick.

"Move your laptop so I can see you better," Kyle demanded in a husky voice.

The angle of the computer screen allowed Kyle a view of everything. It might be kind of embarrassing but hotter than hell, so Rory allowed the view.

Kyle moaned. "Nice body. God, look at your cock. The things I want to do."

He swallowed and then asked, "Like what?"

"Like suck you. Trace your finger around the crown. Yeah, just like that. That's what I'd do with my tongue."

"Oh fuck." Rory followed Kyle's instruction. His fingertip seemed to morph into Kyle's tongue.

"We could do that too. But first, I want you to stroke your cock in time with me."

Groaning, Rory warned him, "I'm really close."

"Good." Kyle growled and started moving his fist.

Matching the hand pumping on the screen, Rory edged climax. "Kyle!"

"Hands off." Kyle took his hand away.

"Fuck!" Rory throbbed. A strong gush from the heating vent would have made him come. He panted. "You're killing me."

Kyle smirked. "Just want to make it last." He inhaled and exhaled harder than usual. "Ready?"

"No stopping this time, right?"

The mischievous smile worried Rory, but Kyle said, "Right. Ready, set, stroke nice and slow."

Rory followed the command.

"That's right... enjoy it for me, Rory." The breathless cadence of Kyle's words licked parts of Rory that were ready to give Kyle whatever he wanted. "Pretend it's my hand on you, going up and down. Yeah, a little faster."

Rory kept time by staring at Kyle's hand. Everything in him coiled tighter. His toes curled as he tried to hold on to the pleasure that was threatening to break loose. "Kyle."

"Yes, Rory. Come." Kyle's cock erupted and a white stream rained down on him and the bedding.

"Kyle!" Rory groaned as satisfaction burst free from his core. Waves of bliss radiated outward, releasing all his frustrated impatience.

Kyle gave him a crooked grin and stared at him from the computer screen. "That was awesome."

"Best Valentine's Day ever." That had to be the greatest thing that ever happened to him.

Kyle snagged his cell from his nightstand and frowned at it. "Hey, you have class soon, but do you wanna meet me here later to celebrate more?"

Rory used his sheet to wipe his mess. "Definitely. I'm done by three o'clock."

"I'll see you at 3:05." Kyle laughed. "Seriously, why don't we plan to eat together and—"

"Via Skype?"

"Yeah, why not? Pick up something to eat, and we can... hang out."

Like a real date? Rory didn't ask, but it sure felt like one. "Cool. I'll text you in a bit."

CHAPTER 5

The time passed with incredible slowness, and counting down to BishounenCon didn't help. Though they'd repeated their Valentine's Day date more than once over the past month. Truth be told, every day started with a jerking session with Kyle via Skype to cheer him on to orgasm.

Finally, Rory paced around his duffle bag in the hotel lobby, holding his BishounenCon badge trying to breathe.

Did he and Kyle really have something? Skype, texts, and emails were one thing, but what about in real life? Doubt crept in. And what happened at the end of this weekend?

Rory had dreamed about the kiss that never was for the last five months and thirteen days... *God!*

Fingers combed through Rory's hair, and then a hand wrapped into the hair at the nape of his neck. Forcibly spun, he was dipped.

Oh God!

Rory exhaled, and his body tightened with anticipation. "You came."

"Not yet... but we will." Minty breath tantalized Rory's lips. The words barely registered before soft lips glided against his mouth.

Finally!

Kyle slid his lips gently across Rory's mouth again and again. Then he nipped at Rory's lower lip until he parted his lips and let Kyle push his tongue inside, insisting Rory kiss back.

Yes!

At last, he kissed the man who twirled his world off its axis. The kiss was everything he'd fantasized it would be—and so much more. Rory's entire body surged with arousal.

More. His arms wreathed around Kyle's neck, and he deepened the kiss. Their connection twined tighter, locking them together. Giggling from other Yaoi fans was the only thing that forced Rory back to the reality of their location. God, he needed so much more!

Kyle grinned at him. "Are you glad to see me?"

A million emotions ranging from terror to *"Fuck me!"* raced through him, but the rainbows of happiness shooting through his brain were the deciding factor. "Yeah... I am."

"Rory...." Kyle's voice tripped wires in Rory's head, making instant lust bubble to the surface. Bringing him upright, Kyle stared into Rory's eyes.

Rory pondered the depths of Kyle's dark gaze, and he

wanted to explore and understand everything about this man. "I can't believe...."

"We're here?" Kyle's deep voice made him shiver.

Damn. Even in jeans and a T-shirt Kyle was hot. "This is the first time I've seen you out of cosplay."

A sexy grin curled Kyle's lips. "No, it isn't."

Every filthy, sexy, incredible moment they'd spent doing pornographic things slammed all the blood Rory had into his cock. He tried to say something other than "um," but nothing made it out of his mouth.

Kyle pulled him into his arms once more. "I didn't take the time to change into costume. I wanted to find you."

The butterflies in Rory's stomach took a victory lap.

They had spent a lot of time together on Skype, texting and whatever, but seeing each other in person was great and terrifying all at once.

Kyle's cheeks tinted pink, and he rested his forehead against Rory's. "I don't want to waste a moment with you this time. Let me take you upstairs, and we can...."

"Um...." He nodded. It was insane. But the clock was ticking, and Rory wasn't going to play hard to get.

Kyle grabbed Rory's duffle bag and held his hand as they rode upstairs in the elevator. Unlike other guys Rory had known, Kyle didn't drop his hand when the door opened to let on more people. He squeezed tighter and smiled brighter.

When the elevator door opened on the seventh floor, Kyle said, "This is us."

Rory allowed Kyle to guide him down the hallway

and into the room. He was so overwhelmed by the generous gift of the weekend, he'd never asked, "Who else are we rooming with?"

"No one. It's just us." Kyle turned the deadbolt, locking them in and the rest of the world out.

Rory should let Kyle know he'd never.... But how? He'd tried to tell him during a conversation on Skype, but the words wouldn't come out, and then the subject had changed.

Pointing to the king-sized bed that dominated the room, Rory shook his head. "I... um... haven't...."

"Never?" Kyle wasn't stupid; he got it. Or maybe Rory had a sign flashing "Virgin" over his head.

A quick check in the mirror confirmed no neon above his head as he slipped the camera off and set it on the dresser. He shrugged. "Well, some, a couple times with girls, but not... with a guy."

"Mmmm, I like that in a very Seme-kind-of-way." Kyle set Rory's bag down and brought Rory's fingertips to his mouth. He licked each finger, then sucked the index finger into his mouth, all the way in.

A strangled sound escaped Rory. The attention went right to his cock. "Um...."

Would this be an inappropriate time to beg for a blowjob?

Kyle skimmed his hands down Rory's body. "We don't have to do anything you don't want, but *God...* I want to be inside you."

What could he say? "Okay?" *Shit!* He didn't mean for it to sound like a question but—

Rory opened his mouth for hot spearmint kisses. Kyle's lips were soft, but his tongue demanded submission. Kyle began to erase some of Rory's worries, and replaced them with a long to-do list.

He tugged off Rory's T-shirt and unbuttoned the jeans that were now way too tight. The zipper slid down, giving Kyle room to slip his warm hands under the jeans and Rory's briefs.

Rory stood there like an innocent uke. Maybe he should say something witty or touch Kyle back, but all that happened when he opened his mouth was a whimper.

Kyle ran his hands against Rory's bare skin and then squeezed. "I love your ass."

Rory swallowed as Kyle kneaded his asscheeks, and then pulled him tighter against him. Hard-on rubbed against hard-on.

Oh fuck! The sensation of need-to-come-now barreled into his dick. Why hadn't he jerked off this morning? *Note to self: never ignore your hard-on before a convention.*

Kyle teased a finger along Rory's crease, hinting at future activities.

Glad for his thorough shower that morning, Rory allowed himself to be guided backward until his legs pressed into the bed. This was happening.

Kyle tugged everything below Rory's waist off. Nothing else mattered but the man in front of him.

Hot breath rushed over Rory's erection, forcing him

to sit on the puffy bedding. Screaming "Suck me off!" would be considered rude, right?

His long-awaited fantasy began to unfold... Kyle on his knees in front of him. Did it get any better than this? Rory's brain started to short-circuit.

Kyle flicked the tip of his tongue over the head of Rory's cock in slow, wet licks. Yes, yes it did get better! Tongue-on-cock contact was definitely superior. "Fuck, that's amazing!"

Grinning, Kyle teased long trails of wet heat from the base of Rory's cock to the top, driving him insane. Each time, he lapped at the drip that appeared from the slit. Drip, lick, drip, lick... again and again.

After an eternity of sexy torture, Rory couldn't take the building pleasure. His patience gone, he begged, "Please...."

The sexy smirk almost pushed Rory over the edge, but he held it together.

The glint in Kyle's eyes reminded Rory of a Seme intent on making his uke lose his mind.

Kyle traced his tongue from Rory's balls to every place along his cock.

Holy fuck! Rory wiggled his lower half, looking for more. Was Kyle taking Seme class? Or teaching it?

Kyle kissed the head of Rory's cock, and then he grinned at him. "You want me to suck you?"

Would anyone actually say no? Voice gone, Rory nodded.

Kyle engulfed the head of Rory's dick into his mouth. The unexpected suction, coupled with licks from Kyle's talented tongue, made Rory grab the bedding. Kyle pushed his mouth down and sucked in half of Rory's length in one go.

Rory's eyes would have rolled back into his head, but he couldn't take his gaze off Kyle. His cheeks hollowed, and his eyes remained locked onto Rory's. The special closeness, the connection he'd experienced on Skype, intensified and wound tighter around them. All he wanted was more.

Kyle pressed down on Rory's thighs to prevent his involuntary hip thrusting. It served to remind Rory who was in control....

Incredibly hot!

Groaning in surrender, Rory tried to be still and let Kyle go at his pace.

Kyle rewarded him with some head bobbing that fucked Rory's cock into his mouth faster.

"God!" Rory craved rushing forward to a climatic conclusion. Their eye contact made him believe he had the strength to endure this plateau forever just so he could remain this close to Kyle.

Earthquakes. Sinkholes. Tornadoes. Rory's dick wasn't up to the challenge of forever, because holding it together for the next thirty seconds seemed impossible. Only thinking of natural disasters stopped Rory from orgasming immediately.

Blowjobs were totally underrated. Why did anyone ever do anything else?

He twined his fingers in Kyle's hair. Rory wanted to compliment Kyle on his incredible skill, but all he managed was tightening his fist, twisting his body, and whining pathetically.

Crinkle. Crinkle. "Fuck!" Kyle pulled off Rory's cock and ducked low out of the line of his vision. The scrunch of plastic coming off a tube, then *snick.*

Soon enough Kyle popped back up, smiling triumphantly at Rory.

The clenching of his heart compensated for the loss of Kyle's mouth and made Rory's toes flex with pleasure. But what had he—

The expression Kyle wore morphed, making him look like a stern Seme. He shoved Rory back flat onto the bed.

"Hell yeah!" Rory groaned. All his dreams of being taken by a dominant man were nothing against the delicious reality of Kyle claiming what Rory offered.

The questions he wanted to ask fled when Kyle's heated mouth returned to his cock. A lubed finger teased his entrance. All thought vanished.

Rory gasped. He'd never played with his ass, so the feeling was kind of weird... odd, though not unpleasant... like a stroking pressure.

Fuck no! It was incredible—like heaven.

"*There.* Right there." Rory tried to communicate that complex thought but could only dig his heels into the mattress and shift around.

The sucking slowed, and Kyle added another finger. He rubbed his digits in and out of Rory.

The enticing tempo created a longing deep inside. "More," Rory croaked as he tried to reach for the pleasure.

Nodding, Kyle squirted more lube onto his fingers and pushed in a third.

Wait! That didn't feel as... oh, yes it did!

Rory whimpered, and made a grab for his cock. His orgasm hovered on the fringes just out of his reach.

"Wait." Kyle stilled his hand.

Rory frowned, and almost asked *for what*, but didn't.

Kyle stood and wiggled out of his jeans. If Kyle looked good with his clothing on... without them... well, that was a view that forced Rory to follow instructions. Rolling a condom on his dick, Kyle smiled with confidence. He coated the length with lube. "You're going to love this."

Before Rory could fully form his thoughts of uncertainty, Kyle pulled Rory's knees up, making room for him to kneel between Rory's legs. He circled his cock over Rory's opening.

All the months of talking, texting, and jerkoff sessions led Rory to this moment. Indecision fled; he wanted this, and he wanted this with Kyle. "Please."

God! Hungry to be filled, Rory adjusted his position, and wrapped his legs around Kyle's ass, trying to yank him forward. He craved Kyle inside him to somehow finalize—as stupid as that sounded—their connection, and he had to have him now.

"Shhh, I got you. Trying not to rush it." Kyle's soft voice attempted to soothe. He pushed the head in.

"Fuck!" That was not a good thing.

Rory's whole body tried to stop the intrusion. The stretching burned. No wonder so many ukes in manga cried out in pain during sex and had a look of misery on their faces. This hurt!

"Relax. Just relax," Kyle cooed.

Easy for him to say. He doesn't have a tree trunk shoved up his ass! Rory shifted, trying to find a more comfortable position, like back on the West Coast. Maybe they should go back to cock sucking. He'd never—

Kyle slid out.

Relief. Was that it? It was over? Well, that was... disappointing. It couldn't be finished. Kyle hadn't come, and neither had Rory.

Kyle added more lube to his cock, then pushed back inside.

Damn, not done.

He stroked Rory's limp cock with his wet hand.

Oh yeah. Definitely not done!

The slippery friction on his dick started to wake feelings of delicious incredibleness. Rory got hard despite the uncomfortable fullness in his ass.

Kyle slid in a little deeper.

Rory gripped Kyle's shoulders. The realization hit him. The man who'd filled him with dreams of yaoified love and happily-ever-after fantasies was inside him.

Kyle stared down at him and gave him a crooked smile.

Rory's heart clenched and expanded with affection. He pressed his lips together so he didn't blurt out his feelings. No, he did the safe thing and simply returned the smile.

"A bit more." Kyle thrust all the way in. He held his body so still, his arms shook and he panted, "You... good?"

"Yeah" came out all broken.

Kyle had become Rory's first.... God, why did his heart want Kyle to be his last? But they lived on different coasts! How were—

"I'm going to move." Kyle's voice broke during the moaned warning.

What? Should Rory move too? Maybe he could—

Kyle tightened his fist and started stroking Rory's cock faster, in time with his thrusts.

Reaching around, Rory rested his hand on Kyle's firm ass. Disbelief shoved out of his head when he caressed Kyle's smooth, round, and wonderfully squeezable asscheeks. This was happening.

Kyle shifted. He wiggled and pushed back into Rory.

Damn! Feelings of affection that had never accompanied sex before were slamming through him. This was more than he'd expected. How could he—

"How's that?" Kyle studied him.

"That's.... *Oh!*" Fire licked through Rory. It wasn't comfortable, but it was kind of good. He started to crave more....

Kyle changed his angle and rocked into Rory.

Yeah, he began to really appreciate the fullness and pressure. He pushed back against Kyle's thrusts.

Leaning down, Kyle pressed his lips to Rory's. His thrusting slowed and found an enticing rhythm.

Rory's hands rode with Kyle's ass. He started pulling him deeper, testing different angles.

There! Yeah, that was interesting.

Why did Kyle's fist loosen around him? The cock-stroking attention stopped midstroke!

After another minute, Kyle exhaled hard and gasped. "I can't—coming."

Kyle pushed in deep and squeezed his eyes shut. His body rippled over Rory's. Kyle's handsome face twisted in torment, and he grunted, finding fulfillment.

He'd left Rory just short of heaven.

No! Dear gods, don't stop!

Rory's whine of disappointment must have reached Kyle in the land of orgasm, because he readjusted his fist and tugged Rory in quick strokes.

Rory's prayers to the gods of Yaoi worked!

Dick hard. Ass full. Close. Close. Yes. Oh God!

Rory came. He tensed his ass muscles around Kyle, making his orgasm radiate outward with more intensity. "Fuck!"

His pleasure was almost painful. Every shot made him clench around Kyle. He shivered and pushed Kyle's hand away when he was finished.

Kyle stopped pumping and squeezed him, finishing off with perfection.

"Ah," Rory sighed. That was.... It had to be the strongest orgasm he'd ever had.

Kyle groaned as he pulled out and collapsed next to Rory.

Ahhh and *ow* mixed together, but emotions overpowered them both.

Rory stared at the ceiling. What should he say? That

had been everything he'd ever thought sex should be. To have this experience with Kyle....

Reaching over, Kyle pulled the comforter around Rory. Then he snuggled Rory closer and whispered, "We'll take a shower in a couple of minutes, but right now I just want to hold you."

Ignoring the clock counting down to the moment they'd have to part, Rory burrowed against Kyle and decided to enjoy the moment.

CHAPTER 6

The dance of the vibrating phone woke Rory from the most peaceful sleep he'd ever gotten. *Where —oh. Mmmmm.*

Rory snuggled into Kyle's body. He rubbed his face in Kyle's chest hair and enjoyed the scent of him... and of them.

"You want to see who that is?" Kyle gestured toward the nightstand.

"Nope." Rory pressed closer to Kyle's warmth and nuzzled his neck.

Kyle chuckled and nabbed Rory's phone. "Here, you should. You've been texts for the last ten minutes."

The hotel room was dark, but Rory wasn't sure if that was the blackout curtains or if it was nighttime. "What time is it?"

Kyle rolled toward the clock and told him what Rory's cell also read. "It's 7:30."

"Wow. I guess we fell asleep after the last time." Kyle

wouldn't fuck him again because he said he didn't want Rory to be too sore. Even though Rory denied it and pouted enough to make any uke proud, just a little shifting of his muscles told him the blowjobs had been the right decision.

"Yeah." Kyle kissed his forehead and left the bed. He handed Rory one of the bottles of water near the empty ice bucket.

Rory gulped down the warm wet liquid. He glanced at his messages. "It's Amber."

"How's Amber?" Kyle and Amber had gotten to know each other through social media, emails, and brief Skype contact.

"As Ambery as ever." Glad it was too dark for Kyle to see his probably very red face. He thrust the cell at him.

Kyle read all of her demanding and embarrassing texts out loud. "R did you get laid? You got laid. Was it good? I told you anal was happy face emoji. Why aren't you texting back? Was it... she used a poo emoji. Tell me. Don't make me call you."

Rory groaned and took back his cell. He typed *Don't you have better things to do than to harass me? Like attending a Saturday night orgy?*

The cell vibrated in his hand. Rory read, *Nope. Orgy doesn't start 'til 9. Do tell.* She added a happy face emoji and the pile of poo emoji with a question mark.

Kyle pulled him back against him and whispered, "So was it happy face emoji or...?"

Dropping his head back onto Kyle's shoulder, he

nipped Kyle's jaw. "I think you know." He sent a triad of happy faces to Amber and showed Kyle.

Rory pressed a kiss on Kyle's mouth. His ass didn't hurt that bad, but Rory's stomach betrayed him with a growl.

Kyle pulled back. "Come on, get dressed. We'll get dinner first, and then we'll just stop into the dance to hear how bad the music is."

Staying curled around Kyle seemed like a much better way to spend the evening. More sex would keep reality at bay.

But who could dissuade a Seme intent on a... dance party?

The music at the dance party wasn't terrible. Bodies gyrated to the beat, then slowed down as if on cue as Kyle and Rory stepped through the door. The lights dimmed, and disco lights spun in patterns to guide the dancers. A soft, sexy melody turned the dark into some black-and-white movie.

"Dance with me." Kyle tugged him out onto the dance floor.

Rory slipped into Kyle's embrace as if he were born to be there. He allowed himself to be guided by the rhythm of Kyle's body pressing against his, easily following.

The lyrics sang of one true love, and even though he mouthed the words, he didn't look at Kyle. This wasn't a

Yaoi with an easy answer. No, this was life, and reality could pretty much suck.

Kyle nuzzled Rory's neck, making him want to head back to the room and forget about... everything other than each other.

"Maybe we could—" Rory tried to wheedle them toward the exit.

Apparently, Kyle wasn't aiding and abetting Rory in his escape plans. Kyle did guide them to a quieter corner of the ballroom and twirled him like a fairy-tale prince.

The light was dim but enough so Rory could see the serious expression Kyle wore. Kyle's tension made Rory nervous. Was Kyle going to say they should see other people? Maybe they should... but—

"I know we haven't spent much time together outside of Skype, but I feel like I know you." Kyle touched over Rory's beating heart and placed Rory's hand over his heart. "And you know me."

Rory nodded. He couldn't agree more and that terrified him.

"I get why you didn't want to talk about the future and all, but I think we should."

Fear ripped through Rory. What was between them was too good to survive in the real world. Distance and time would erode the perfection, so he selfishly wanted this weekend.

"How about we enjoy BishounenCon, and we talk on Sunday."

Kyle frowned and took Rory's face in his hands. He stared deep into Rory's eyes as if trying to share his soul with him. His mouth captured Rory's in a kiss meant for the pages of a Yaoi, not for real life.

Each of Kyle's kisses was precious, and Rory tried to memorize them all. He wanted to save the taste for when there would be no more.

This kiss was soft and full of... affection, for lack of willingness to apply a more accurate descriptor. The brush of Kyle's tongue and the glide of his lips made Rory want to believe that maybe, just maybe, they could have forever.

CHAPTER 7

Late Sunday morning...

The weekend had flown by amid cuddles, blowjobs, snuggles, and more sexual adventures than Rory thought possible. But now it was late Sunday morning....

"Come on. We should shower." Kyle dragged him into the bathroom.

They took turns brushing their teeth and using the toilet. How could activities of daily living be so heartbreakingly perfect?

Rory sniffed, stepping under the spray; he hoped Kyle would think it was the water that made his eyes red.

Kyle joined him. He grabbed the bodywash and soaped up every part of Rory, making him want to get dirty again.

The shower rained down, drenching, but doing nothing about Rory's hard-on other than making his cock wet.

Fuck! Kyle's hair had gotten slicked back and made

him look even sexier. He wore a smile that said Rory was in trouble, and he'd fucking love the dilemma about to befall him.

Whoosh!

"I need you, Rory." Kyle pinned Rory against the shower wall.

The cold tile on his ass barely mattered as Kyle rutted his cock against Rory's until stars burst behind his eyelids. Rory tilted his head so Kyle could suck a mark onto his neck.

Rory's heart clenched. If only Kyle meant that in the way Rory wanted Kyle. Why did they have to live on opposite coasts? It sucked. Pushing away the yaoified dreams of happily ever after, Rory focused on a more practical happy ending. "Here I am."

Dropping to his knees, Kyle demonstrated, for probably the fifth time this weekend, how talented his mouth was by sucking in more than half of Rory. He froze and peeked up.

Rory stared down at the vision that topped his wishes and dreams list. It was surreal, and then Kyle smiled around his cock, taking him to another level of unreal ambitions.

He grabbed Kyle's hair to stay upright as he fell back against the tile. His groan for mercy was met with eyes sparkling full of mischief.

Kyle bobbed his head excruciatingly slowly. He sucked in more of Rory's cock on each descent until he tickled his nose in pubic hair. His mouth ringed around Rory's base, and Kyle swallowed.

"God!" As good as that was, it wasn't enough.

Kyle slid back to the tip. He wrapped a hand around the base of Rory's dick and started to stroke him off with a slight twist as he sucked harder. It was another unique feeling in a weekend of firsts.

"Fuck!" Rory clutched Kyle's hair tighter.

The delicious sucking and twisting tugs got faster... and that was it!

"Kyle!" Everything good in the world converged making Rory come hard. He pulsated in time with Kyle's strokes and sucks.

Kyle stayed on Rory's cock until he swallowed everything. Rory caught his breath as aftershocks of pleasure cascaded through him. Long licks helped guide Rory back from the land of grunting orgasms.

Standing, Kyle nuzzled Rory's neck, and steadied him.

Rory moaned in blissful contentment. He slumped against Kyle, and allowed him to support his weight. As their breaths synced, Rory wished their feelings would as well, but—

Kyle's erection bumped into Rory's leg.

Oops! Rory had basked in release, forgetting Kyle suffered. He kneeled at Kyle's feet. "Let me taste you."

He licked Kyle from tip to base and back again.

"Oh man! You've gotten good at that." Kyle leaned against the wall and combed his fingers through Rory's hair.

"It's all the practice you've given me." Rory licked him like a lollipop. He dragged his tongue up along the shaft and swiped around the tip to capture all of Kyle's sweet precome. Then he flicked his tongue around the crown again and again.

Kyle slapped the wall with his hand. "Please, Rory?"

"Please what?" Having found his inner uke, Rory discovered he enjoyed tantalizing his Seme.

"Put me in your mouth... just a little," Kyle begged in a very non-Seme way.

Rory loved the vulnerability, and fucking hell, he loved Kyle. He couldn't confess this truth out loud, but yeah again the inconvenient truth reared trying to steal the happiness of now. Dread of the future heartbreak almost overwhelmed him, but he focused on giving the best blowjob the world had ever seen. He sucked like he could change the future.

Kyle shook and groaned like he'd been shot. "That's it, Rory. Yeah, just like that. Suck me."

Hollowing his cheeks added enough suction to make Kyle moan. Rory wrapped his hand around Kyle's cock, and stroked the length that wasn't in his mouth at the speed he found Kyle enjoyed the best.

Kyle's head thumped against the wall.

Rory took him in as deep as he could without gagging. He bobbed his head and used his fist the way Kyle had.

"Yeah! So good! Suck me off, Rory," Kyle gasped.

Adoring the desperate sounds Kyle made, Rory figured he must be doing something right, so he continued.

A grunt and a strangled "Swallow" was the only

warning Rory got before his mouth filled with the salty taste of Kyle. He sucked harder and did as instructed.

Gratification at making Kyle lose control fulfilled him. He'd put that satisfied smile on Kyle's face.

When Kyle's orgasm finished, he pulled Rory off the floor and into his arms for a movie kiss.

The joy of necking made rainbows colored with happy endings and yaoified happily-ever-afters dance through his heart—

"I should get you something to eat, and we should double-check your flight."

Until reality stomped in.

Rory pressed his lips to Kyle's and clung even though soon enough they'd go back to their separate coasts, shattering his Yaoi fantasy of their happily ever after ever being possible.

Shifting in the high chair at the hotel's sports bar, Rory couldn't find a comfortable way to sit. It had been a busy weekend.

Kyle grinned but thankfully didn't comment. "I'm starving. How about you?"

The weekend ending made Rory not hungry, but he said, "Um, yeah. I'll have whatever you're having."

Waving the waitress over, Kyle ordered burgers with fries and two Mountain Dews.

Turning his attention to Rory, he asked, "So, it's Sunday, and we've never really talked about your plans?"

The waitress brought the sodas.

"My plans?" Rory swallowed hard. This was it.

"Yeah, like what are your plans with school, work... you know, everything?"

Rory did know what he wanted wasn't on offer. "Actually, after I graduate in two years with a BA, I'm hoping to get my Masters in social work from San Francisco State."

Kyle's eyes widened. "Wow. That's awesome."

"Yeah, you'll be graduating sooner, though. What about you?" That sounded like a normal question one would ask a friend, fuck buddy, and the love of his fucking life. Rory ripped off a piece of his napkin and shredded it into tiny bits.

"Well, I'm planning to accept a job offer in San Francisco." Kyle studied Rory.

What? Hope ricocheted through him. "Really?"

"Yeah, I'll start in June. There's a big need to work with LGBT youth in the city, and I decided since I have a boyfriend there—"

"Excuse me?" *What the fuck?* They'd been skyping for months, and after this weekend they did every sexual thing imaginable... some things twice! And now Kyle was fessing up about a boyfriend?

"You.... You're there. I'm moving there because I want to be with you. If that's okay...?"

What? "Yes... that would be fine." He was sure every desperate emotion, elation, and relief he felt transmitted with no need for translation.

Kyle grabbed the hair at Rory's nape and pulled him

into a crushing kiss. When he moved back, Kyle whispered, "I know this maybe is too soon, but I love you, Rory. I want to be with you. I'm going to do my best to make all your dreams come true."

The promise of yaoified love was infused in each glide of Kyle's lips.

Rory soared with the possibilities of their future together. His heart was too full. He pulled back and stared through blurry eyes. So many things he wanted to say, but he settled for "I like when real life is like a Yaoi."

"Me too. I got us a late checkout. Come on, we still have a couple of hours...."

Rory asked for their food to go.

CAUTION — OVER THE TOP!

WARNING: This Epilogue is completely over-the-top, and a double dose of Yaoified love. It may not be suitable for all audiences. Continue reading at your own risk.

TWO YEARS LATER...

Amber kept the entire graduation ceremony from being a snorefest with her texts.

Kyle looks handsome.

Yeah. Rory left out he looked even better this morning when they'd traded blowjobs.

She texted, *It's good your parents like him.*

They like him better than me.

LOL

Your row is up. Shake with your right, accept with your left.

Rory pocketed his cell and stood in line. Four years of hard work, and it all morphs into a piece of paper. Though the paper, his grades, and several professor recommendations got him a full ride including a sweet teaching assistant gig for grad school. So, he wasn't in a position to complain.

And since Kyle's apartment was close to SF State, they'd be living together officially. For the last year or so, he'd been staying over Friday through Wednesday. Maybe he could put aside his hatred of Wednesday and Thursdays nights now.

Rory jogged up the steps to the stage. As his name was called, he searched the audience one more time, but couldn't find Kyle. He smiled at his waving parents.

He shook hands with the dean, accepted the scroll, and moved his tassel to the other side of his goofy-looking hat. Unexpected relief rushed him. He'd done it. Searching the crowd, he wanted to share the moment with Kyle.

Where was Kyle? Why wasn't he with his parents?

As he walked off the stage, he stared at the seat Kyle had just been sitting in all morning. His foot hit the floor and a flash caught his attention.

White cards held by people in the section above where his parents sat spelled R-O-R-Y.

More white cards came into view and were flipped over. W-I-L-L Y-O-U M-A-R-R-Y M-E? I L-O-V-E Y-O-U K-Y-L-E

Oh my God!

Kyle appeared in front of him holding a red velvet ring box. "Rory, I love you. Your parents have given me their blessings. Please say yes and marry me."

"Yes!" Rory pulled Kyle into a kiss.

Some of the crowd who were aware of, and in on, the proposal broke into thundering applause, causing a minor disruption in the ceremony.

Kyle rushed him through a side door and they escaped into a courtyard.

Rory laughed.

"What?" Kyle pulled him into his arms.

Rory kissed Kyle's lips and then said, "That was wild and wonderful and the biggest yaoified gesture ever."

"You liked it?" Kyle asked as if there was a way Rory wouldn't appreciate such an effort.

Sometimes, reality could be awesome. He squeezed Kyle tight and proclaimed, "I love when real life is like Yaoi."

Kyle gave him a bone-melting smile. "You mean the hot sex or the happy endings?"

Tilting his head, Rory played the uke and asked, "I have to choose?"

His Seme growled and assured him, "As long as you're with me, you'll get both."

ABOUT THE AUTHOR

Z. Allora believes in happily ever afters for everyone. She met her own true love through the personals and has traveled to over thirty countries with him. She's lived in Singapore, Israel and China. Now back home to the USA, she's an active member of PFLAG and a strong supporter of those on the rainbow in her community. She wants to promote understanding and acceptance through her actions and words. Writing rainbow romance allows her the opportunity to open hearts and change minds.

Find Z's Books at:
Rocky Ridge Books
Dreamspinner

Find Z. around the web:
www.zallorabooks.com
Z.AlloraHappyEndings@gmail.com

ALSO BY Z. ALLORA

Opposites might attract, but is acting on that attraction wise?

Librarian Tristan Cooper can't steer clear of sexy, motorcycle-riding bad boy Phillip—the man is hot—but Phillip is bound to find quiet, bookish Tristan boring, like all Tristan's boyfriends. Tristan yearns to explore the wild side of himself. Maybe rakish Phillip is just what he needs to feel free.

Sexperienced hairdresser Phillip is more of a believer in happy endings than happily ever afters. He's learned not to hope for more—until he meets sweet, vulnerable Tristan, who seems genuinely interested in his heart. But Phillip can't imagine Tristan might want him for more than a night.

With the help of a pair of matchmaking grandfathers, Tristan and Phillip might find the courage to step beyond their comfort zones and discover what's missing from their lives.

Rejected. Heartbroken. Devastated.

Zack Davis wanted to serve only one man, Andrew Nikeman. He was denied for what Andrew thought were good reasons. So Zack crushed his submissive tendencies and focused on being the perfect Dom, giving every sub he played with something he couldn't have.

After years of denying his submissive side, Entwined's charity auction "Are you Dom Enough to be a sub?" gives Zack an excuse to get a little of what he's always craved.

Andrew doesn't know when his infatuation turned into more, but it kills him to see Zack with a constant parade of submissives. He'd refused to jeopardize his brother's relationship or become Zack's regret; however, Zack isn't a kid anymore, and his brother's relationship is unbreakable. Now Zack's popularity and success as a Dom might ruin Andrew's dreams of collaring him, but he can't wait any longer to confess his feelings or he risks losing the man he loves forever.

Buy at Dreamspinner or your favorite retailers.

More Goodies from Z.

THE DARK ANGELS
TIED TOGETHER

Z. ALLORA

THE DARK ANGELS
FINALLY FALLEN

ROCKY RIDGE BOOKS   K ANGELS

Z. ALLORA

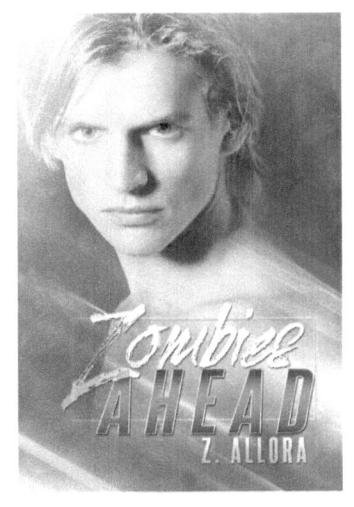

Zombiez
SUCK
Z. ALLORA

Zombiez
COMING
Z. ALLORA

Keep current with Z.'s doings (and the whole Rocky Ridge gang) by joining the newsletter.

www.ingramcontent.com/pod-product-compliance
Lightning Source LLC
Chambersburg PA
CBHW020543130626
46552CB00007B/2739